Charm Hall

Charm Hall

AND COMING SOON

Charm Hall

Midnight Mayhem

Tabitha Black

Hodder
Children's
Books

A division of Hachette Children's Books

Special thanks to Sue Mongredien

For Hannah Powell, with lots of love

Copyright © 2007 Working Partners Ltd
Created by Working Partners Limited, London, W6 0QT
Illustrations copyright © 2007 Margaret Chamberlain

First published in Great Britain in 2007 by Hodder Children's Books

2

A Catalogue record for this book is available from the British Library

ISBN 978 0 340 93141 7

Typeset in Weiss by Avon DataSet Ltd,
Bidford on Avon, Warwickshire

Printed and bound in Great Britain by
Clays Ltd, St Ives plc

The paper and board used in this paperback by Hodder Children's
Books are natural recyclable products made from wood grown in
sustainable forests. The manufacturing processes conform to the
environmental regulations of the country of origin.

Hodder Children's Books
a division of Hachette Children's Books

Chapter One

"Good morning, girls!"

"Good morning, Miss Collins," Paige Hart
replied, along with everybody else in the room. It
was a hot day, and her form group were about to
start their English class. A bumblebee was droning
outside the open classroom window, and Paige
could hear the *thwack* of tennis balls coming from
the courts. Paige blew a stray red curl out of her
eyes and fanned herself with her exercise book.
Summertime had definitely arrived at Charm Hall
boarding school, that was for sure!

Miss Collins turned to chalk something up on

the blackboard, and Paige smiled as she saw her friend Shannon Carroll crane her neck to see what the teacher was writing. That was Shannon all over: she hated being kept in suspense. Paige's gaze drifted over to Summer, who was staring into space in a world of her own. Her two best friends were like chalk and cheese but Paige wouldn't have had it any other way.

She had only been at Charm Hall a short while, but it already felt like home. So much had happened since she'd said goodbye to her parents several weeks ago! *Let's see*, Paige thought to herself. *Since Mum and Dad moved to Dubai with Dad's new job, I've started a new school, made two brilliant new friends, and met a mischievous kitten, Velvet, who just happens to be magical!*

"I have a special announcement to make this morning," Miss Collins declared, turning to face the class.

Paige switched her attention back to her teacher to see that Miss Collins had written *A Midsummer Night's Dream* on the blackboard. Paige's class had been studying the Shakespeare play since the beginning of term. Paige wondered what Miss Collins was about to tell them.

"As you are the youngest students at Charm Hall, you may not know that it is a tradition at our school for one year group to put on a summer play at the end of term," Miss Collins said. "It's quite a big occasion, with the whole school invited to watch, and parents, too, of course. And I'm pleased to tell you that this year, the Year Fives have been chosen to act, direct and produce the play." She smiled and pointed at the blackboard. "And yes, you're going to be putting on *A Midsummer Night's Dream!*"

"Cool!" exclaimed Shannon, with a big smile at Paige and Summer.

Paige felt a rush of excitement. "This is going to be fun!" she whispered, and Summer grinned.

Everyone in the class was talking excitedly about the news. Paige really liked the play, with the fairy king and queen, and Puck the mischievous fairy. And she loved all the funny bits, like when Bottom the weaver got the head of a donkey!

The class hushed as Miss Collins began talking again. "I'll be holding auditions for parts in the play at the beginning of next week," she told them. "But, as well as actors, I'll need students to work behind the scenes too: making costumes, painting scenery, operating the lights and sound effects . . . all sorts of things. I'll also need an assistant director and a stage manager."

Abigail Carter's hand shot up. "Please, miss, what will they do? The stage manager and assistant director, I mean."

Miss Collins smiled at the keen look on Abigail's face. "The assistant director will be working with me, to guide the actors through their performances," she replied. "And the stage manager will be responsible for organizing all the behind-the-scenes activities. Things like overseeing the props and sets, and running the backstage and onstage areas during the show."

Shannon was looking particularly interested, Paige noticed. She smiled. Out of the three friends, Shannon was definitely the bossiest, in the nicest possible way, of course! Paige could tell that the idea of organizing a whole play really appealed to Shannon.

"If anybody is interested in any of the behind-the-scenes roles, do come and speak to me directly," Miss Collins went on. She smiled around the classroom, her eyes shining. "There will be something for everyone to do, and we're all going to have great fun!" she said. "But before anything else, we'd better finish reading the play, so if you all turn to Act Four, Scene One, we'll find out what happens next."

Paige flicked through the pages of the play, a big smile on her face. She loved painting and drawing, and she was already thinking about doing something creative for the play. Scenery painting sounded good. She was looking forward to talking to Summer and Shannon about it at lunchtime.

After their English class, Paige and her friends headed for the dining hall to get lunch.

"Putting on the play is going to be great," Shannon said happily. "Which parts are you two thinking of trying out for?"

Before either Paige or Summer could reply, Abigail Carter barged past them. "Of course, I'll get the assistant director role," she was boasting loudly to her friend Mia. "Miss Collins gave me a really high mark for my last essay on the play, and even said that I clearly understood the workings of

A *Midsummer Night's Dream* really well," she said, sounding very confident. "It's obvious I'll get to direct. And with your background, Mia, you're bound to get the role of Queen Titania!"

Paige and her friends joined the queue for food behind Abigail and Mia, and Shannon rolled her eyes at Abigail's comments.

"What does Abigail mean, 'with Mia's background'?" Paige asked curiously, keeping her voice low.

"Mia's mum is a famous actress," Summer explained in a whisper. "Diana West."

"Yeah. I reckon that's why Abigail doesn't boss Mia around as much as she does everyone else," Shannon added quietly. "She probably loves the idea of being friends with Diana West's daughter."

The three friends collected their food and sat down to eat.

"Forget Abigail and Mia, anyway," Paige said. "What are you two going to try out for? I'd quite like to help out with the set design, especially if I can paint the backdrops."

Shannon twirled some spaghetti around her fork. "I'd love to be assistant director," she admitted, and then her eyes flicked over to the next table, where Abigail was still talking about herself in a loud voice. "Although Miss Carter over there seems to think she already has *that* job in the bag."

"Don't be so sure," Summer said. "Miss Collins is good at seeing straight through Abigail's sucking up."

"And you'd make a great assistant director," Paige added. "You're brilliant at bossing people around – and as your roommates, we should know, right, Summer?"

Shannon pretended to look shocked and then laughed, but Summer was staring into space.

"Summer?" Paige repeated. Her friend seemed very thoughtful all of a sudden. "What are you thinking about?"

Summer bit her lip. "The thing is, I'd love to be Puck," she confessed, "but . . ."

"But nothing!" Shannon told her. "You'd make a fabulous Puck!"

Summer shrugged. "I'm worried I'll get stage fright," she said. "I don't know if I even dare audition."

"You should go for it," Paige told her encouragingly. "I think you'd be fantastic."

Summer's cheeks had turned pink. "Thanks," she said shyly, "but I'm not sure. Don't tell anyone I'm thinking about trying out for Puck, will you?" she added hastily.

"Don't worry," Paige reassured her friend. "You should know by now we're all experts at keeping secrets." She forked some tuna from her salad into a napkin, so that she could sneak it upstairs as a treat for Velvet. Then she grinned and added quietly, "Especially *kitten*-sized secrets!"

Chapter Two

"Oh, it's no good!" Summer wailed. "I'll never get this right. Why am I even trying?"

It was Sunday afternoon, and Paige, Shannon and Summer were up in their attic bedroom with Velvet. The kitten was snoozing at the bottom of Paige's bed and Paige and Shannon were keeping Summer company as she practised her lines for the audition that was on Monday. Paige looked over sympathetically as Summer slumped down on her bed.

"I just can't get Puck's personality right in my head," she complained. "*That's* why it's coming out wrong."

"Try it again," Shannon said encouragingly. "I think you're doing fine."

Summer stood up again, took a deep breath and started reading. *"Thou speakest right; I am that merry wanderer of the night,"* she declared. *"I jest to Oberon and make him smile . . ."*

Paige watched her friend. Summer's bright-blue eyes lacked their usual sparkle and her forehead was creased in anxious lines as she read Puck's words. She didn't look like she was having much fun.

"And sometimes lurk I . . ." Summer's voice trailed away. "Maybe I should give up," she sighed. "At breakfast, I heard that Harriet Morris from Swan House is trying out for the part of Puck, too. I'm sure she'll be much better than me."

"Don't give up!" Paige said. "Honestly, Summer, you can do it."

But Summer had already tossed the book on to her desk. She sat down on her bed with a sigh. "I don't think I can," she replied. "I just can't get a clear image of Puck in my mind."

At Summer's words, Velvet stretched and woke up. Then she got up from where she'd been sleeping and bounded across to Summer. She put a gentle paw on Summer's hand, looking up at her with wide amber eyes.

"Hello, Velvet," Summer said lovingly, as Velvet started to rumble with tiny purrs. "Did you come to cheer me up, then?"

Velvet gave a little chirrup, as if she was agreeing.

It's just as if she can understand everything we say, Paige thought with a smile, as Summer tickled the kitten under her chin.

Then Velvet jumped down off the bed and sprang up on to Summer's desk, where the copy of *A Midsummer Night's Dream* lay open. Velvet sank down on the desk, her gaze fixed on the book as if she were stalking it. Her black tail flicked from side to side behind her.

Paige watched with interest. You never knew what was going to happen next when you shared your room with a magical kitten!

"You just have to believe in yourself," Shannon was saying to Summer. "And don't worry about Harriet Morris. She—"

"Look at Velvet!" Paige interrupted. "Something weird is happening."

Velvet had her nose pressed to the open book and her whiskers were vibrating and shimmering with a magical golden light. As the girls watched, bright golden sparks shot from Velvet's whiskers, bounced over the pages of the book, and then whizzed away around the room.

Paige held her breath as the leaves of the book now began to flutter rapidly backwards and forwards as if caught in a strong breeze. Then, all of a sudden, a tiny winged boy burst from the pages and zoomed up into the air in a shower of golden sparks.

"What is *that*?" Shannon asked, staring at the boy with wings as he zipped around the room.

"It's a . . ." Summer began, staring. "It's a *fairy*!"

The girls watched, open-mouthed, as the fairy whizzed over their heads and then flew in a nosedive straight towards the floor. Just when Paige thought he was certainly going to crash into the carpet, he stopped dead, and then popped up in front of the girls, bowing and grinning.

"Good day, maidens!" he cried cheerily. "I am Puck!"

"The merry wanderer of the night!" Summer

breathed, her eyes as round as marbles.

Puck looked pleased by her words, and bowed again. "The merry wanderer himself," he declared. He gazed around the room, looking excited and bemused at the same time. "But where has the wood gone?" he asked. "What is this place?" He darted closer to the girls, his eyes sparkling eagerly. "And why is it that I am here?"

"I . . . I . . . don't know," Shannon stammered.

"I think maybe it was something to do with our kitten," Paige added.

"She may have done something magical to my book," Summer put in shyly.

Puck looked over at Velvet who was now sitting up on Summer's desk, washing her front paws, and nodded wisely. "Cats are very magical creatures. It has always been so," he said seriously, and then he turned a backflip in the air and a cheeky grin came over his face. "But if there is nothing here for me to do, then I shall fly!" he announced, hopping on to the window sill. "Maybe I can have some fun before King Oberon notices that I am gone. Farewell!"

"Wait!" called Paige, jumping to her feet.

But before the girls could stop him, the mischievous fairy had zoomed straight out of the open window and disappeared.

Chapter Three

Paige rushed to the window and stared out. There was no sign of Puck anywhere. "Quick! We've got to find Puck before anyone else spots him," she cried.

Summer nodded.

"Come on!" said Shannon, throwing open the door.

The three girls ran downstairs and outside. Charm Hall was surrounded on all sides by lush green lawns and colourful flower beds that led to leafy woodland. Paige looked around worriedly. *Puck really could be anywhere by now!* she thought anxiously.

It was late afternoon, and there were lots of other students around. Some were sunbathing on the lawns, some were playing tennis, others were just hanging out under the trees. Paige, Shannon and Summer tried to look casual, and not at all as if they were scanning the gardens for a tiny, fast-moving fairy!

After several minutes of searching, the girls reached the terrace that adjoined the dining hall. Paige noticed Abigail and Mia sitting at one of the picnic benches, deep in conversation.

"Spotted him!" Shannon hissed, looking pointedly at the ground near Abigail and Mia's bench.

Paige looked . . . and immediately saw Puck. He was under the bench tying Abigail's and Mia's shoelaces together! "You two distract Abigail and Mia," Paige whispered, as they approached the bench. "I'll try to catch Puck."

"OK," Shannon whispered, slapping a big fake smile on her face and walking over to the girls. "Hi, you two. What have you been up to today?"

Paige ducked down and pretended to tie her own shoelace as Abigail launched into a lengthy monologue about why *she* didn't need to go for an audition because she had already told Miss Collins what she wanted to be . . .

"Puck!" Paige snapped as quietly as she could. "Stop that!"

Puck gave a guilty start and swung round to look at Paige.

"Untie those shoelaces," Paige said in a warning voice, "and go back to our bedroom straight away. Otherwise, I'll . . ." a flash of inspiration struck her, ". . . I'll tell King Oberon and Queen Titania exactly how naughty you've been!"

Puck pulled a sulky face, but he undid Abigail's and Mia's knotted shoelaces and tied them up properly again. "I do not wish the king and queen to know of this," he muttered, "so I will return to your room. Farewell!" And with that, he zipped high up into the air, until Paige could only see a tiny dot in the sky.

"Paige?" said Mia suddenly. "What are you doing down there?"

Paige froze. *Thank goodness Puck has gone!* she thought. "Um . . . just tying up my shoelace," she said brightly. She got to her feet, brushing the dust off her skirt. "Hi, guys," she said. "How are you?"

"Fine," Abigail replied at once. "In fact, better than fine. If you must know, Miss Collins has practically promised me the assistant director's role." She tossed her long, honey-coloured hair over one shoulder.

"What do you mean?" Summer asked.

"Yes, what did she say?" Shannon put in.

"She said that my role would be central to the success of the whole play," Abigail said, with her nose in the air. "Sounds to me like she's already picked me for the assistant director!"

Paige saw Shannon's face fall. "Not necessarily," Paige said quickly, determined to stop Abigail's boasting. "Miss Collins didn't say for sure that you have that role."

"Yes, she said she would allocate all the roles *after* the auditions," Summer reminded Abigail.

Abigail didn't look especially bothered by this. "Well, I know what she was trying to say to *me*," she replied. "I got the message loud and clear!" She smiled at Mia. "And as Mia is sure to get the part of Titania, it looks to me as if Peacock House is going to do very well in the play! How do you think Hummingbird House will do?" she added sweetly. Paige knew Abigail was well aware that she, Summer and Shannon were all in Hummingbird House.

"We'll do just fine, thank you," Shannon said, turning on her heel and walking away.

Paige and Summer followed. Paige could feel herself bristling with annoyance. It was so infuriating the way Abigail took every opportunity to show off!

"What happened with Puck?" Summer asked, when they were out of earshot.

"I threatened to tell the fairy king and queen about how naughty he'd been if he didn't fly straight back to our dorm," Paige replied with a laugh. "So he's gone back there."

"Let's go and meet him then," Shannon suggested, breaking into a jog. "We don't want him on the loose again, do we?"

"Definitely not," Paige agreed. "He's just as naughty in real life as he is in the play!"

Up in their bedroom, to Paige's relief, Puck was waiting for them. He was fizzing about impatiently.

Like a bad-tempered bluebottle, Paige thought, shutting the door behind her.

Velvet was curled up on Paige's bed, keeping a watchful eye on the fairy, her little black ears pricked up as she watched him buzz about.

"I'm bored!" Puck moaned, turning somersaults and backflips in mid-air. "And hungry, too. Being here is no fun."

"Would you like some chocolate?" Shannon offered. She pulled open her desk drawer and brought out a bar of milk chocolate. She broke off a small piece and held it out for Puck.

Puck flew over to her palm and picked up the chocolate curiously. "I have not come across 'chocolate' before," he said, taking a nibble. He smiled as he bit off a second mouthful. "Heavenly!" he declared, greedily finishing off the rest. He bowed low before Shannon. "Thank you."

"You're welcome," she smiled, sharing the rest of the bar out between them all.

Paige, who had the feeling Puck was something of an entertainer, suddenly had an idea for keeping him amused. "Shall we play charades?" she suggested. "Puck, you can go first. You have to act out a word, and the rest of us will try to guess it."

Puck's eyes brightened. Then he screwed up his face as he thought for a moment. "Very well," he said at last. "This is my word."

The girls watched as Puck shut his eyes in concentration, and then hurtled up into the air in a shower of sparks. There was a loud bang, and then Puck went whizzing about the room, sparks still shooting out all around him, before he soared gracefully to the ground once more.

Velvet's eyes were as round as saucers as she watched this display.

"A firework!" Summer laughed. "Your word must have been 'firework'!"

Puck beamed proudly and did a celebratory backflip. "You are correct," he told her, his eyes sparkling. "Thou speakest right; I am that merry *firework* of the night!"

Summer laughed. "Cool backflip, Puck," she said admiringly. "I wish I could do them like that."

"Your backflips are the best in our year," Paige told her, with a grin. "You're just being modest, Summer!"

The dinner bell rang just then, and Paige

reluctantly got to her feet. "We can't miss dinner, or we'll be in trouble," she said, frowning as she wondered what to do with Puck.

"What will you do while we're downstairs?" Shannon asked him suspiciously.

Puck gave an airy shrug. "Oh, do not trouble yourselves about me," he said. He put on an angelic expression and perched on the edge of Shannon's desk. "I'll just sit here patiently and await your return," he assured them, then gave a cheeky wink. "As long as you bring me some more chocolate . . ."

"OK, we'll see what we can do," Paige told him, laughing. "And we won't be long – so don't go anywhere!"

The three girls waved goodbye to Puck and then clattered downstairs to the dining hall. Paige tried to eat her dinner as quickly as possible because she was anxious to get back to the little fairy. Although Puck had said he'd wait patiently for them to get back, he hadn't struck her as a very patient sort of person. She couldn't help wondering what mischief he was making upstairs, while they ate!

Shannon and Summer must have felt the same,

because Paige noticed that they also rushed their meal. Luckily, dessert that night was an ice cream with a chocolate flake sticking out of the top, so Paige and her friends wrapped the flakes in a napkin, for Puck, and Paige slipped the chocolate into her pocket before they all ran back upstairs again.

Their room was right at the top of the school building, up three flights of stairs, and Paige was sure she had never run up them as quickly as she did now. "Puck!" she panted, flinging open the bedroom door as they reached their attic room. "We're back! And—"

Paige stopped short, taking in the peaceful bedroom, the open window, and Velvet, who was looking up at the window from Paige's bed. The kitten miaowed meaningfully at the girls.

"He's gone again, hasn't he?" Shannon said, rushing into the room.

Paige nodded and sank on to her bed with a groan. "Where has he disappeared to now?"

Chapter Four

"He must have got bored," Summer sighed, going over to the window and peering out. "We should have known he wouldn't be able to stay out of trouble for long!"

"Well, we've got to find him," Shannon said, stroking Velvet. "I wish you could tell us where he's gone, Velvet!"

Velvet purred throatily in response and rolled on to her side to have her tummy tickled. As she rolled over, Paige noticed that Velvet had been sitting on a library book.

She smiled. "You're a funny little thing," she said,

leaning over to stroke Velvet too. "That can't have been very comfortable!" She picked up the book, noticing as she did so that it was due back to the library that very day. "I'd better take this back to the library," she said, frowning. Then she smiled and shook her head. "But first things first – right now, we have to go on another fairy hunt!"

"Unfortunately for us, Charm Hall is very big, and Puck is very small," Shannon grumbled an hour later. The girls had looked all around the school grounds, and were now searching every nook and cranny inside the school itself: the classrooms, the gym, the assembly hall, the computer room . . .

"We must have walked miles," Summer said. "Where could he be?"

Paige remembered her library book which she'd been carrying around while they searched for Puck. "We haven't looked in the library yet," she suggested. "And I need to go there anyway, to drop off this book."

"OK," Shannon agreed, following Paige.

The girls made their way to the library. Charm Hall was something of a maze with its long corridors and twisting staircases. Paige remembered how often she'd got lost when she had first started at the school. Sometimes, she still had to think twice about which way to go.

As they approached the library, Paige noticed a strange greenish light coming from beneath its heavy wooden door. She broke into a run. "Look," she said. "Is it just me, or does that light look kind of . . ."

"Magical?" Summer finished for her. "It certainly does!"

"Oh, no. What do you think he's doing in there?" Shannon muttered. "Please don't let anyone have spotted him!"

They rushed to the door and flung it open. Paige gasped as she saw Puck whizzing through the air like a tiny firefly. He was darting from shelf to shelf, peering closely at the books. Paige scanned the rest of the library quickly, checking to see if anyone else was around. Thankfully, apart from Puck, the room seemed to be empty.

"What's he doing?" Shannon whispered with a frown.

They all watched as Puck heaved a book off one

of the shelves into his arms. It was so heavy, it almost dragged him to the floor, but puffing and panting under its weight, the little fairy dragged the book through the air to the nearest table. Then he opened the book, and pointed at the pages, his face alight with a cheeky smile.

Paige's eyes widened as a magical-looking green mist swirled from the fairy's fingertips and flowed over the book. What *was* Puck up to?

Puck chuckled to himself in a satisfied sort of way, and then zoomed back towards the bookshelf, leaving the book on the table.

"Puck!" said Shannon, stepping into the library. "What's going on?"

At her words, the fairy jumped, then grinned mischievously. "I am making the books more fun," he replied, hopping from one foot to the other in mid-air.

"What do you mean?" Paige asked, stepping into the library too. She noticed that there were a lot of books on the table. Had Puck pulled *all* of them off the shelves?

Puck shrugged. "I mean that I have taken the dull books and I have made them more . . . interesting!"

With a sinking feeling, Paige picked up one of the books from the table. *The Fall of the Roman Empire,* the title read. She flicked to the first page and read out loud, " 'What's brown and sticky? A stick!' "

"Jokes?" Summer asked in horror.

Paige flicked to another page. " 'What do you get if you cross a witch with a snowstorm?' " she read aloud. " 'A cold spell.' "

She glared at Puck. "You've filled this history book with jokes!" she cried.

Puck nodded proudly. "Good, aren't they?" he asked.

"No!" Summer said. "They're terrible!" She was flipping through a geography textbook. " 'What do vampires have every morning at 10.30?' " she read out. " 'A coffin break?' Oh, Puck, these aren't even *good* jokes!"

Shannon suddenly giggled. "This one's quite funny, actually," she said, reading another book. " 'What goes haha bonk?' " she read, chuckling. " 'A man laughing his head off!' "

Puck grinned. "I like that one, too."

Paige shook her head at the cheeky fairy. "You'll have to change the books back, Puck," she said. "And then come back with us, where we can keep an eye on you."

Puck shook his head stubbornly. "The books are much better now," he said. "Look," he added, pointing to a corner of the library. "That maiden fell asleep, her book was so dull!"

"Which maiden?" Paige asked in alarm. She turned to see where Puck was pointing – and gulped. There in the corner, fast asleep at the table and almost hidden by a stack of books, was Harriet

29

Morris – Summer's rival for the part of Puck!

Paige stared at the sleeping girl in horror. If Harriet woke up and saw Puck, or the joke-filled books, there would be some serious explaining to do. They had to get Puck to return the books to normal, and then get the naughty fairy out of there at once! But how? Puck had looked very stubborn when Paige had asked him to change the books back. She had to think of a way to persuade him to undo his magic . . .

Suddenly, Paige remembered the chocolate in her pocket. She took out the flakes and unwrapped them, then waved one in the air. "If you don't change the books back right now, you won't get any of this lovely chocolate," she said in a fierce whisper.

Puck licked his lips, and stared longingly at the chocolate.

"I mean it!" said Paige, sensing that Puck was tempted.

Puck's bottom lip slid out in a sulky way. "All right," he said reluctantly. With a last look at the chocolate, he began flitting from book to book, muttering and pointing his finger at each one. As he did so, a green mist swirled around each book and their pages fluttered softly.

Summer picked up a book and checked it. "It's fine," she said. "Well done, Puck."

Puck made a rather bad-tempered little bow. Then he glanced over to where Harriet was snoozing. "There is one more book that must be changed," he said. "But the maiden is sleeping upon it."

The girls exchanged a worried glance. Harriet's head was resting right on the book's open pages.

"We can't let Harriet see Puck," Summer said.

"Definitely not," Paige agreed.

"Puck, do you think you can use your magic to change the book back *without* disturbing Harriet?" Shannon asked.

Puck glanced again at the chocolate in Paige's hand. "I will try," he said hesitantly.

Paige bit her lip as the fairy flew over to where Harriet was sleeping. He landed lightly on the desk near Harriet's arm and pointed at the book. Paige held her breath as the green mist swirled around, but Harriet remained asleep.

Paige sighed with relief as Puck turned to leave, but just then, a coil of mist drifted right under

Harriet's nostrils. Harriet's nose twitched irritably in her sleep and then she sneezed.

"Oh, no!" Paige said under her breath. *Please don't let Harriet see Puck*, she thought, crossing her fingers behind her back. *Please!*

Paige watched as Harriet stirred, blinked and then jumped as she found herself looking straight at a smiling fairy!

Chapter Five

"Hello, maiden," said Puck with an impish bow, followed by a series of cartwheels and then an impressive backflip. "I'm Puck!"

"I . . . I'm Harriet," Harriet stuttered in confusion.

"Pleased to meet you, Harriet," the fairy replied politely. "I'm sorry I woke you. I shall not disturb you any longer." And, with a final wave, Puck zoomed out of the library window.

"Quick, let's get out of here as well!" Shannon whispered. "Before Harriet spots *us*, too!"

Shannon and Summer both bolted out of the

library door, unseen, and Paige turned to follow, but it was too late.

"Paige!" cried Harriet.

Paige grimaced and stopped. "Sorry, Harriet, got to go," she blurted out. "It's almost time for lights out!" And before Harriet could say another word, she raced out of the door, and ran all the way back to the dorm.

Puck was apologizing to the others as Paige burst in. "It was not my intention to make mischief," he said earnestly. "I was just having fun."

"Well, it wasn't much fun for us," Paige said, slightly out of breath but trying to sound stern. She handed him the chocolate. "Here you are."

Just then, the sound of silvery chimes rang out from Summer's copy of *A Midsummer Night's Dream*.

"What was that?" Shannon asked, peering at the book suspiciously. "Don't tell me another fairy's going to pop out now!"

Puck shook his head and licked chocolate from his lips. "King Oberon calls me," he explained, with a little bow. "I go, I go, look how I go, swifter than arrows from a bow."

Paige smiled, recognizing the words from *A Midsummer Night's Dream*.

"Puck, are you really going?" Summer asked.

Puck crammed the last of the chocolate into his mouth and did a very elaborate set of cartwheels over the girls' heads. Then he made a deep bow and said, "Indeed I must! Goodnight unto you all!" And with that, he zoomed towards the book and dived straight into its pages.

"Goodbye!" Shannon cried, as Paige dashed over to the book and flicked through the pages. Puck had vanished.

Just then, there was a knock at the door, and Harriet put her head around it. She was still looking rather shell-shocked, Paige thought.

"Where is he? Where's Puck?" Harriet demanded.

Paige, Shannon and Summer exchanged a worried glance. *How are we going to get out of this one?* Paige wondered.

"What?" Shannon replied, clearly trying to sound as innocent as she possibly could.

Summer gave Paige a sneaky wink. They both knew what Shannon was doing. "Puck?"

Summer queried looking confused.

"What are you talking about?" Paige asked Harriet, wide-eyed.

Harriet looked doubtfully from one girl to another. "I was in the library," she said slowly, "and I dozed off. And then, when I woke up, I saw Puck – the fairy from the play. And you, too, Paige."

"In the *library*?" Paige asked, trying to look astounded.

"You must have been dreaming," Summer said helpfully.

"No, she's trying to wind us up," Shannon put in. "Like we're going to fall for that one, Harriet! Fairies in the library indeed!"

Harriet looked a little sheepish, and shook her head. "I'm spending too much time thinking about this play," she said with a sigh. "I'm even *dreaming* about the characters now!"

Harriet left the room and Shannon closed the door with relief. "Phew!" she sighed. "That was close. Having Puck around was definitely exciting – but a bit *too* exciting for my liking!"

Paige nodded and sank down on to her bed just

as Velvet bounded in through the window. "Hello, puss," Paige said, stroking her. "You've just missed Puck – although I guess you knew that already, right?"

Velvet gave a little mew and climbed on to Paige's lap.

Shannon watched. "I wonder why Velvet conjured him up in the first place," she said thoughtfully.

Summer smiled and came over to stroke the little cat. "I think *I* know," she said mysteriously, then headed for the bathroom. "I'm going to get ready for bed now," she added, changing the subject. "It's a big day for me tomorrow – audition day!"

Shannon grinned at her. "So you're going to try out for Puck, then?"

Summer nodded, a determined look on her face. "I'm going to sign up for the audition first thing in the morning!" she declared. "I know exactly what Puck's like now."

On Monday afternoon, after lessons had finished for the day, Paige and Shannon went with Summer to the assembly hall. They were keeping her company while she waited to audition. The try-outs for the part of Titania were just beginning as they sat down. There were three girls auditioning for the role: Priya Dutta, Lizzy McLean and Mia West. Paige and her friends watched them with interest.

Lizzy and Mia both did well, but Priya put in an excellent performance. As her clear, confident voice rang out across the stage, Paige could really imagine her as the fairy queen. *Even Puck would be in awe of her*, Paige thought with a smile.

"She was good," Summer whispered after Priya had finished.

Paige squeezed Summer's hand. "You'll be great too," she told her.

Miss Collins walked on to the stage. "Thank you, ladies," she said. "Next, the part of Puck. Harriet, would you read first, please? And then you, Summer."

Paige watched Harriet intently as she stepped up. She stood centre stage and read her lines loudly and clearly. She wasn't bad, Paige thought critically, but she wasn't entirely convincing. She just didn't have any of the cheekiness and energy that they'd seen in the real Puck.

And then it was Summer's turn. "Good luck!" Paige and Shannon said together as she made her way towards the stage. Summer flashed them a quick smile and waved.

"She's not half as nervous as I thought she would be," Shannon remarked in a low voice.

Paige nodded and grinned at Shannon as Summer walked to the edge of the stage. "I think I'm more nervous than Summer is," she joked in a whisper.

Summer stood very still to one side of the stage for a moment, then she did two cartwheels to take her right into the middle. Everyone gasped. She finished her last cartwheel with a spring into the air, and grinned at the audience. "Thou speakest right!" she declared. "I am that merry wanderer of the night!" She tumbled into a backflip, and the audience let out another gasp.

"I jest to Oberon, and make him smile," Summer went on, with a wink at the audience.

"She's brilliant!" Paige whispered in delight.

"Just like Puck!" Shannon whispered back.

Summer turned in a fantastic performance. She made the stage her own, filling every corner of it

with tumbles and making everyone laugh with her reading of Puck's jokes. When she'd finished, there was a moment's silence – and then the whole hall erupted in applause.

"Look at Miss Collins," Shannon murmured, nudging Paige happily.

Paige glanced over to see Miss Collins clapping her hands and smiling delightedly at Summer.

As Summer made her way back to Paige and Shannon, Harriet rushed up to congratulate her. "It was just like seeing the Puck I dreamed of!" she confided. "Well done. You really deserve the part."

Summer blushed. "Thank you," she said. "You were good, too," she added.

"That was amazing," Paige said to Summer as they went back up to their dorm, for Summer to change back into her uniform. "You didn't look nervous at all!"

Summer blushed. "It was meeting Puck for real," she explained. "I could remember my lines easily when I imagined him speaking them. And seeing the way he darted about, with his backflips and cartwheels, gave me the idea of putting some in my performance."

Shannon hugged her. "I always knew all that gymnastic training would come in handy!" she said happily.

Summer grinned. "It wasn't just the gymnastics," she said. "I need to thank a certain little kitten, too."

"Velvet is so clever, she must have known exactly what you needed," Paige agreed.

They'd reached their bedroom by now, and Summer pushed the door open. Velvet was waiting for them expectantly on the end of Summer's bed.

"Thank you, Velvet!" Summer cried, running over to make a fuss of her. "I couldn't have auditioned without you! Now I just have to hope that Miss Collins gives me the part."

Chapter Six

The next morning, the list of cast and backstage roles was pinned up outside the English classroom. The whole of Year Five crowded round to see who'd been chosen for each part. Paige, Summer and Shannon slipped in where they could.

Paige scanned the list for scenery painters. *Alice Hayes, Louisa Bridges and Paige Hart*, she read. "Hooray! I'm a scenery painter. Just what I wanted!" she cheered.

Just then, Summer let out a little scream of excitement and clutched Paige's arm in delight. "Look!" she cried, pointing at the list with a trembling finger.

Paige read: *Puck – Summer Kirby*. "Well done!" she cried, hugging her friend. "You did it!"

Then Shannon let out a great whoop and started dancing around on the spot. "I got assistant director!" she yelled, trying to hug Paige and Summer whilst still dancing.

Paige couldn't stop grinning. They'd *all* got what they'd wanted!

"*What?*" came a furious voice at that moment, and Paige turned to see Abigail, looking aghast as she stared at the board.

Ouch! Paige thought, remembering how much Abigail had wanted the assistant director role too.

But Abigail suddenly brightened as she spotted her name. "Hey! Stage manager!" she cried. "I'm stage manager!" She tossed her hair over one shoulder. "Definitely the most important role in the play," she added. Then she turned expectantly to Mia, who was beside her. "So – are you Titania, then?" she asked.

Mia looked rather white-faced. She just about managed to shake her head before she ran off in tears.

Paige watched her go, then looked back at the

list. No, Mia hadn't been chosen to play Titania. Priya had got that role instead. Mia was in the costume design team.

"Mia, wait!" Abigail called, running after her disappointed friend. "Mia! Come back!"

Preparations for the play began the following week. Everyone was buzzing with excitement as they began learning lines, ordering props and designing the set. The costume materials were delivered, as were the paints and backdrops, and all the Year Five girls got to work.

The play was going to be performed in the assembly hall, which had its own stage and curtains, and the largest drama room, just next to the hall, was to be used for set designing. This was where the props and costumes would be made, and the scenery painted.

In *A Midsummer Night's Dream* there were scenes set in the palace, the forest and Quince the carpenter's house, so backdrops and scenery were needed for all of those locations. That added up to a lot of painting, but Paige was loving every minute of it! It was such fun to work on a large scale, rather than being restricted to pieces of paper, as she usually was in art class.

Together with Alice and Louisa, the other scenery painters, Paige often went to work on their backdrops after school. With the radio on, and the costume designers and prop makers busy alongside them too, there was always a fun, friendly atmosphere. Paige was pleased to see that Mia seemed to be enjoying her role of costume designer. She was really good at it, too! It was clear that Miss Collins had known just what she was doing when she'd given Mia that job.

One afternoon, the three scenery painters were working on some of the trees together. Paige was enjoying painting with Alice and Louisa. Alice had a great sense of humour, and Louisa was very creative. Together, they made a good team.

Just then, Summer popped her head around the door. "Hi, guys, have you seen my wings anywhere?" she asked. "I tried them out yesterday to check I could still do my backflips with them on, and I'm sure I put them back in the cupboard afterwards, but . . ." She shrugged, looking puzzled. "Well, they're just not there any more."

Paige shook her head. "I haven't seen them, sorry," she said.

"Nor me," Alice piped up, and Louisa shook her head.

Summer called across to Mia, who was cutting out material for a fairy costume. "Have you seen my wings anywhere, Mia?"

"Your wings? No I haven't," Mia replied, frowning.

Summer sighed anxiously. "I hope they aren't lost," she said. "I wonder where they could be."

Summer went off to look again, but when Paige saw her later that evening, the wings still hadn't turned up. It was very odd, thought Paige. Summer wasn't a forgetful sort of person.

The next day, Paige and the other backstage artists were hard at work again, when Katie Scott, who was playing the part of Bottom the weaver, came in and started taking everything out of the props cupboard. "Has anyone seen my donkey mask?" she fretted. "I know I put it back in the costume cupboard, but it isn't there now." She sighed as she gazed at the empty shelves of the props cupboard. "And it isn't in here either," she added, piling the props back in. "Any ideas?"

Paige shook her head, along with the others. "Sorry, Katie," Paige said sympathetically. "Did you leave it onstage?"

Katie ran a hand through her unruly black curls. "Nope," she sighed. "It's just vanished!"

At the end of that day's rehearsal, Miss Collins called the whole production team together. She asked the group about the missing wings and donkey mask, but nobody had seen them.

Miss Collins sighed. "Please could everyone make sure that they return all their props and costumes to the cupboard after rehearsals?" she asked. "The fairy wings and donkey mask can be replaced, but I don't want anything else to go missing. We've got a lot of work to get through before we can put this play on. Having to make things twice over because of carelessness wastes everybody's time!"

Summer was very tense as she, Paige and Shannon went up to their room afterwards. "I feel awful about my wings," she sighed. "I was so sure I had put them back in the cupboard. I must be going mad!"

"Don't be too hard on yourself. You've got a lot on, with all your lines and gymnastic moves to practise," Paige said. "And it's not like you're the only one to lose anything – Katie did too."

Shannon was looking thoughtful. "You know, Summer, you're probably the most organized person I've ever met," she said. "You never lose anything."

"Oh, thanks," Summer said, rolling her eyes. "Make me feel worse, why don't you?"

"I'm not trying to," Shannon told her. "I'm saying that I find it really hard to believe that you *did* lose your wings." She paused. "And don't you guys think it's odd that Katie's donkey mask has gone missing, too?"

Paige frowned. "What do you mean?" she asked.

"What I mean is this," Shannon said, looking grave. "What if the wings and mask weren't lost? What if they were *stolen?*"

"Stolen?" Summer echoed.

"Think about it," Shannon urged. "There's definitely something odd going on here. I don't think the fact that two things have gone missing is just a coincidence."

Summer sighed thoughtfully. "It's possible," she said cautiously.

Paige nodded. "But who would want to steal them?" she asked.

Shannon shrugged. "I don't know," she replied. "That's what we've got to find out."

Chapter Seven

"I have some news to report," Miss Collins said a few days later. She had called the play team together for a progress meeting in the hall, and her face was serious. "This morning, while Ellie Douglas was searching for a script, she found Puck's wings and Bottom's mask."

"Oh, thank goodness!" Summer burst out, looking enormously relieved. "Where were they?"

Miss Collins's face was stony. "That's the strange thing," she said. "The wings and mask were found together in the theatre bin. They had been cut into pieces and then thrown away."

There was a shocked silence. Paige stared at her teacher in disbelief. Cut into pieces? Thrown away like rubbish?

"But . . ." Shannon's voice broke the silence. "But who would have done that?"

"And *why*?" Summer added. She was looking very upset at the news of her broken wings.

Miss Collins's expression was grim. "I have no idea," she said. Her eyes were like searchlights as she gazed at all the girls' faces. "But I intend to find out. I am very disappointed to think that a Charm Hall girl could have done such a selfish, destructive thing. And if anything else like this happens, I will have no choice but to cancel the play."

A gasp ran around the room, and Paige turned to her friends in shock. This was awful! Everyone had put so much work into the production and letters had already gone out to the students' parents, inviting them to come and see the play. Paige had received an email from her mum just that morning to say that her parents would be flying over from Dubai especially to see it.

"Miss Linnet will speak to all the pupils in assembly tomorrow morning, to remind everyone how hard we are working on the play," Miss Collins went on, "and that acts of vandalism will not be tolerated in this school." She took a deep breath and then forced a smile. "So that's the bad news. Now, let's focus on the positive side of our play, and see how everyone's getting along."

Paige could hardly concentrate as Abigail

launched into a long progress report. She really hoped that whoever it was that had broken the wings and mask wouldn't do anything else to spoil the play. There was no way she wanted it to be stopped before it had even really begun!

The following day, after tea, Paige went to the drama room to carry on with her painting. It was a warm evening, and Summer and Shannon were outside playing tennis before their rehearsal started, but Paige wanted to finish the bush that she'd started painting during lunch.

The room was quiet and empty. Paige guessed that the others were all outside enjoying the last of the day's sunshine. As she walked over to the painting area, she stopped in surprise. Someone had left a wet paintbrush lying in a puddle of red paint on the floor, and Paige picked it up curiously. "Alice? Louisa?" she called, looking around. It was easy to miss somebody if they were painting behind a large piece of scenery.

But nobody answered her. There didn't seem to be anybody else about.

"So who left this here?" Paige muttered to

herself, looking at the mess. She knew Miss Collins wouldn't be pleased at the puddle of paint on the floor.

Dust sheets had been draped over the finished scenery. Paige grabbed one, figuring that she could use it to mop up the spilled paint. But as the dust sheet uncovered a set of painted trees, Paige let out a gasp of shock.

"No!" she breathed, staring in dismay. The trees that she, Alice and Louisa had spent hours working on had been covered with red paint. Paige couldn't believe it. They were ruined!

She pulled off another dust sheet, and another, only to see the same thing. Somebody had splashed red paint all over the backdrops, ruining the scenery.

"What's happened here?" demanded a shocked voice, and Paige whirled around, the wet paintbrush still in her hand, to see Abigail staring at the vandalized artwork.

Abigail's eyes widened as she saw Paige standing there holding the brush. "Paige, what have you *done?*" she asked, open-mouthed. "You've ruined your own work!"

Paige was so taken aback by Abigail's accusation

that for a moment she didn't know what to say.
Then the words poured out. "No, no, I haven't," she
protested. "Why would I want to do that?"

Abigail shook her head, her mouth a tight little
line. "Nice try," she said, "but I don't believe you.
And I'm going to tell Miss Collins what you've done
right now!"

Abigail ran off, leaving Paige feeling stunned.
She could hardly take in what had happened –

finding the paintbrush, discovering the ruined artwork, and then Abigail assuming that *she* had destroyed the scenery! And yet, Paige could see how guilty she must have looked to Abigail, standing there with the wet paintbrush in her hand. And now Miss Collins was going to get involved. Her heart thumped in alarm and she dropped the paintbrush in horror. What on earth was she going to do?

As Paige stood there, panicking, she heard a little *miaow*. She looked down to see Velvet padding into the room towards her. The kitten wound herself lovingly around Paige's legs and batted a paw at a lace that was trailing from Paige's shoe.

Paige gave a small smile and bent down to stroke Velvet, but she couldn't help glancing around nervously as she did so. Miss Collins and Abigail could arrive at any moment, and she didn't want them to see Velvet.

"What are you doing here?" Paige murmured, tickling the kitten under her chin. "You'd better hide before you're spotted." She looked around. Luckily there were a lot of good hiding places nearby. "How about if I sneak you behind this scenery?" she suggested, reaching down to pick Velvet up.

But Velvet was too quick for her. The kitten went springing towards the pool of red paint on the floor.

"Oh, no, not over there!" Paige cried, following. "You'll get your paws all covered in paint!" *Miss Collins will be here any second*, Paige thought frantically, *and how am I going to explain a little trail of red pawprints all over the floor on top of everything else?*

But Paige stopped in her tracks as Velvet's whiskers began to twitch and then shimmer with the magical golden gleam Paige was beginning to know so well. Paige held her breath as the little cat sat down in front of the large pool of paint, her tail swishing back and forth. And then, to Paige's astonishment, the pool began to shrink smaller and smaller, until the spilled paint had completely disappeared!

Then, as Paige stared in amazement, the splashes of red paint on the forest backdrop began to sizzle and flare, as if they were burning up. Bit by bit, the paint disappeared in a dazzling display of red sparks, like tiny fireworks, until the greens and browns of the trees and bushes were visible again,

as perfect as when they had first been painted.

A few moments later, it was as if there had never been any red paint at all, even the paintbrush on the floor was spotless.

Velvet gave a pleased-sounding *miaow*, then scampered across the room to play with a stray bead she'd spotted on the floor near the costume-making area.

"Velvet, how did you—" Paige started, then broke off as she heard footsteps approaching.

"Quick! Hide!" she whispered to the little cat.

Velvet was stalking the bead, her nose almost to the floor, but at Paige's words, she pricked up her ears and hopped into the costume cupboard out of sight.

She really does seem to understand everything, Paige thought, smiling to herself.

"What's all this I've been hearing?" Miss Collins asked as she and Abigail walked briskly into the room. "Paige, what's been going on?" Her voice trailed away as she stared around at the perfectly painted scenery. Then she frowned and turned to Abigail. "But I thought you said all the scenery had been ruined?"

Abigail's face dropped. "But it *was*! There was red paint everywhere – all over the place! And Paige was standing there with a . . ."

"With this?" Paige supplied sweetly, picking up the clean brush.

Abigail's mouth fell open. "But—" she spluttered in confusion.

"That's enough, Abigail," Miss Collins said shortly.

"But—" Abigail protested.

"That's *enough*!" Miss Collins snapped. "I'm really disappointed in you, making such a fuss about nothing!"

Paige couldn't help feeling a tiny bit guilty at the stricken look on Abigail's face. After all, Abigail had actually been telling the truth to Miss Collins. She decided to speak up. "Miss Collins, Abigail was right, there *was* some red paint on the backdrops, but I managed to get rid of it," she said.

Miss Collins glanced from Paige to the scenery, and nodded approvingly. "Well, it looks fabulous now," she said. "You, Alice and Louisa are really doing an excellent job here, Paige. Keep it up!" She turned to Abigail, still looking displeased. "And now, let's leave Paige to get on with her work."

"Yes, miss," Abigail said quietly, her gaze still fixed on the scenery as if she couldn't quite believe what she was seeing.

Paige had to try hard not to giggle. Poor Abigail. And clever Velvet!

Shannon and Summer were both involved in

rehearsals that evening, so Paige didn't get a chance to tell them about the paint panic until the girls were all in bed, after lights out.

Shannon gave a low whistle as Paige finished her story. "Sounds to me like someone is *definitely* trying to sabotage the play," she said. "Nobody would have splattered red paint around unless they were deliberately trying to wreck your work, Paige."

"We'll have to keep watch over the drama room," Summer said. "Remember what Miss Collins said – the play will be cancelled if something else gets spoiled. We can't let that happen!"

"I agree," Paige said. She wriggled under her quilt, not feeling at all sleepy. "We could take it in turns to patrol the hall. We could even have night-time stake-outs!"

Velvet, who'd been curled up at the end of Summer's bed, lifted her head at Paige's words and mewed. Then she jumped lightly to the floor and trotted over to the bedroom door.

The girls all sat up in their beds. The moon was shining through the curtains and they could see that Velvet was standing on her back legs, sniffing at the door.

Paige swung her legs out of bed, feeling excited. "I think Velvet wants us to start our night-time stake-outs right now," she said, and Velvet gave a loud *miaow* as if in agreement.

Shannon pulled on her dressing gown. "Then let's do it," she said decisively. "Mrs Bloomfield has finished her rounds for the night, so come on. Let's go!"

Chapter Eight

"I'll bring my mobile," Summer said, grabbing it from her dressing table. "It's got a little torch in it."

"Good idea," Paige whispered, opening the door.

Velvet darted out of the room and the three of them followed the kitten down the corridor.

Downstairs, the hall was dark, but there was just enough moonlight shining through the large windows for the girls to be able to see. Paige shivered. Being here after bedtime was creepy!

First, the girls checked out the hall, tiptoeing

between the chairs and peering into all the shadowy corners. There was nobody there.

"Right, now for the drama room," Shannon whispered, leading the way.

Paige and Summer followed. The drama room – cheerful and colourful by day – was silent and shadowy by night. The girls crept around, checking that everything was as it should be and looking behind all the scenery. Again, nobody was there, and the room was silent and still.

Paige gazed down at Velvet who was stalking a ball of fluff in one corner. "Velvet seemed so sure that we should come here," she whispered. "Do you think we should hang around for a bit, to see if anything happens?"

Summer and Shannon agreed, so the three friends crouched down behind a stack of boxes, a few metres from the costume rack and props cupboard. Velvet trotted after them, and curled up in Paige's lap.

Shannon suggested a game of alphabet shopping to pass the time. "I went to the market and I bought . . . an angry alligator with ample ankles," she began in a low voice.

Summer giggled. "Alligators don't have ankles!" she whispered.

Shannon grinned. "This one does. Your turn," she declared. "You have to remember what I bought, and add something else, beginning with B, OK?"

The game went on for a while. Paige was just about to start on Q, when Velvet suddenly pricked up her ears and then jumped off Paige's lap. She cocked her head as if she was listening.

Then they all heard it: approaching footsteps! The girls huddled together in silence, crouching low so that they wouldn't be seen.

Paige held her breath as the footsteps drew nearer and nearer. She peeped over the top of the box and saw a girl enter the room. She was dressed in black and carrying a torch. It was too dark to see her face, but she wasn't very tall, and Paige guessed that it was a girl of around her own age. The girl came right up to the costume rack, and pulled Titania's dress off its hanger. Then she snatched up a pair of scissors and began hacking the dress to shreds!

Paige's mouth fell open in shock. Mia had spent

ages working on that dress! She opened her mouth to speak, but Shannon put a warning hand on her arm, stopping her just in time.

"It's too late to save the dress," Shannon reasoned in a tiny whisper. "And we don't want whoever it is to run off before we've found out who they are. We need another plan!"

Summer was rummaging in her pocket. "I can take a photo of her with my phone!" she hissed.

Shannon nodded eagerly.

"Brilliant idea," whispered Paige.

Summer popped up like a jack-in-the-box, and snapped a quick photo while the mystery girl was still hacking at the dress. Then she ducked down again, to show the others.

To Paige's disappointment, though, the picture was too dark for the girls to see the person in it.

"Not enough light," Summer whispered. "I'll try once more, but I don't think it will work." She bobbed up above the box once more, phone in hand. This time, as she did so, Paige saw Velvet's whiskers twitch and start to shimmer with their magical golden gleam. The gleam got brighter until Velvet's whiskers were shining so radiantly that they lit up the whole room.

There was a cry of surprise from the mystery girl as the room lit up and Summer took her photo. Then, a moment later, Velvet's whiskers dimmed and the room fell dark again.

Paige popped her head above the box to try and catch a glimpse of the mystery girl, but she was already racing out of the room.

Summer seemed shaken.

"Did you see who it was?" Paige asked her, as the friends came out of their hiding place.

Summer hesitated. "I think so," she replied, "but . . ." She shook her head. "No, it couldn't have been who I thought it was. Not *her*. We'll have to look at the photo in a good light to be sure."

The girls went over to see if they could find the ruined dress, but it wasn't there. The girl had taken it with her.

"We'd better go back to our dorm," Shannon said, scooping up Velvet and stroking her thoughtfully. "Come on. Let's go before we get caught."

The girls crept swiftly back upstairs. Paige's heart was pounding after their night-time adventure. She'd been shocked to see someone deliberately destroying the dress that Mia had worked so hard on, but now at least they would find out who it had been.

Back in the safety of their room, Shannon put Velvet down gently on Summer's bed while Paige switched on one of the lamps. Then all three friends crowded around Summer as she pressed a button on her phone to display the photo.

Paige gasped as the image appeared on the small screen and she leaned forward for a closer look. She could hardly believe what she was seeing, but the picture left no room for doubt: the girl in the photo was Mia!

Chapter Nine

Paige felt tired the next morning. She, Shannon and Summer had stayed up late the night before, puzzling over why Mia would have wanted to spoil the very dress she'd spent so long making. Clearly, she wanted to sabotage the play, but *why?*

"Maybe it's because she didn't get the Titania role," Summer guessed. "It was Titania's dress that she destroyed."

But Paige had shaken her head. "She's been enjoying designing and making the costumes, though," she pointed out. "She's seemed really happy."

"We'll just have to confront her in the morning,"

Shannon had yawned. "Mia's the only person who can answer our questions."

Now Paige rubbed her eyes sleepily, and looked around the breakfast tables, hoping to spot Mia. Her gaze fell upon Abigail, whom Mia usually sat with, but this morning Abigail was with Katie and Ellie.

"Mia's not here," Summer said, seemingly reading Paige's thoughts. "We'll have to speak to her between lessons sometime." She hesitated, stirring her cereal distractedly. "You know, I'm starting to think I dreamed the whole thing now. It seems so unlikely!"

"I know," Shannon said, munching a piece of toast. "But it definitely happened." She wiped a crumb from her mouth with a thoughtful expression. "It's English first this morning, isn't it? Let's try and catch Mia before the lesson starts."

Paige nodded. "We've got to find out why she's been destroying stuff," she agreed. "And Mia's going to have to tell Miss Collins the truth."

When the girls went to their classroom, though, Mia was already in her seat and Miss Collins was there, waiting – and she was not in a good mood.

Once all the girls were sitting down, Miss Collins held something up. "I found this on my desk this morning," she said.

A gasp went around the room. Miss Collins was holding up the ruined Titania dress. Even Paige and her friends were shocked, despite already knowing it was spoiled. It looked even worse in broad daylight. Mia had hacked through every seam, and the gauzy material hung in shreds.

"I'm sure you all recognize what this is," Miss Collins said grimly. "Or rather, what it *used* to be."

Paige stole a look at Mia who was staring at the spoiled dress as if she was as surprised as everyone else.

"Titania's dress!" Louisa cried out in shock. "It's ruined!"

"I'm afraid so," Miss Collins said, casting a sympathetic look at Mia. "I'm so sorry that somebody has selfishly spoiled all your hard work like this, Mia," she added.

Mia looked down at her desk, an uncomfortable expression on her face. And Paige guessed that she was feeling pretty guilty.

Miss Collins was tight-lipped. "If I don't find out

who did this by the end of the day, then the play will be cancelled," she announced. "And that's my final word on the subject!"

A groan went around the room. "But we've worked so hard on the play!" exclaimed Katie, looking close to tears.

"My mum and dad have taken time off work specially to come and see it!" Abigail protested.

"Who did it?" Ellie Douglas asked, glaring around the room. "If anyone knows anything, they should own up, right now!"

"Hang on, Ellie," Alice put in quickly. "It might not be someone from our form group. Not everyone who works on the play is here."

"Settle down, class," Miss Collins said, putting the torn dress on her desk. "I've asked the other teachers to tell the other Year Five forms of my decision. Now, let's not waste any more of our time on this depressing incident. Turn to page seventy-three of your textbooks, please, and start working through the comprehension exercise there."

Paige's mind was racing as she opened her book. They had to talk to Mia and make sure that she owned up to what she'd done as soon as possible – otherwise the play would be called off. There was no way she wanted *that* to happen!

After lunch, Summer nudged Paige and Shannon. "Now might be a good time," she suggested, indicating Mia, who was strolling out of the dining hall alone.

"Yes," Paige agreed, getting to her feet at once.

Shannon cast a reluctant look at her uneaten strawberry pudding, and then followed the other two over to Mia.

"Mia," Paige called. "Have you got a minute?"

Mia stopped walking, and smiled as the three girls caught up with her in the corridor. "Sure," she said. "What is it?"

"We know it's you," Shannon said bluntly. "We know you ruined Titania's costume."

Mia took a quick, nervous breath, and her eyes widened for a second. Then she squared her shoulders. "I don't know what you're talking about," she declared.

"Oh, yes, you do," Paige told her. "And if you don't own up to Miss Collins by the end of the day, then we'll tell her ourselves!"

Mia gave her a cold look. "Well, you can do what you like," she said, "because I haven't done anything I need to own up to."

"You have," Summer countered. "And we can prove it. I've got a photo on my phone that shows you tearing up the dress!"

Mia turned very pale, and stood there for a second, her mouth opening and shutting in disbelief. Then she stalked off, wrapping her arms around herself as she went.

"I hope she does the right thing," Paige said, watching her go.

"She's got to!" Shannon said. "Surely she can see that she has no choice?"

The bell rang to signal the end of the lunch hour, and the girls went to collect their books for their afternoon lessons. They couldn't help lingering in front of a big poster that someone had put up advertising the play.

Paige winced. "Let's hope that doesn't have to be taken down," she muttered.

The girls climbed the stairs to their dorm, but when they got to their bedroom door, Paige was surprised to see that it was wide open. Worse still, when they went inside, it was clear that the room had been ransacked. Drawers had been pulled open, their contents strewn across the beds, and things had been knocked off the desks on to the floor.

Summer ran straight over to check the drawer in her bedside table. "My phone's gone!" she cried a moment later. "Someone's taken it!"

The girls looked at each other. "Mia," they chorused.

"She'll have deleted the photo by now, I bet you," Shannon added gloomily. "She must have come in here, found the phone and run off with it to get rid of our evidence."

Summer shook her head. "Well, she won't be able to delete the photo," she said, crossing her arms. "It's password protected."

"Summer, that's brilliant!" Shannon said delightedly.

Paige snatched up her maths books and headed out of the room again. "Yes, but we've got to find Mia right now, before she decides to just destroy the phone. Come on!"

Chapter Ten

They ran back downstairs and over to the maths room, only to see Mia walking into the classroom with Abigail and Chloe.

Summer hesitated. "What are we going to do now?" she asked.

Shannon glanced at her watch. "It'll mean we're late for maths, but I think we should sneak into Mia's room and see if we can spot the phone anywhere," she said. She cocked her head towards the classroom. "We've just seen Mia and both her dorm-mates go in there, so we know her room is empty. What do you say?"

Summer wrinkled her nose. "She's probably got the phone with her," she reasoned. "I doubt she'd leave it lying around in her room."

Paige shook her head. "Not necessarily. You know what Mrs Stark's like about mobiles. She hates them, and she has a sixth sense for when one of us has got one in class instead of leaving it in our dorm. Mia would be absolutely mad to take Summer's phone into maths. What if Mrs Stark confiscated it and somehow saw the picture?"

"Come on, let's check out Mia's dorm, then," Summer said. "We've got to at least *look*. My phone is our only bit of evidence. Nobody is going to believe that Mia tore up that dress she made without proof."

The girls turned and headed back upstairs towards Mia's dorm room.

"And if the phone *isn't* there," Paige said, thinking aloud, "we'll just have to confront Mia after maths. We've got to make her tell the truth about this!"

Shannon was first to reach the dorm that Mia, Abigail and Chloe shared. She opened the door cautiously and stepped inside.

Paige and Summer followed and all three girls

quickly started looking for Summer's phone. Paige noticed a framed photo of Mia and her mum on one of the desks and guessed that it was probably Mia's desk. She crossed the room to search it.

As she did so, she suddenly noticed a little furry face outside the window. "Look, it's Velvet!" Paige exclaimed, letting the kitten in. "Come to help us, have you, sweetie?"

Velvet chirruped in greeting and jumped down from the window sill on to Mia's desk. She pounced on a pen, rolling it with her paws. Paige tried not to let Velvet's cute antics distract her. They had a phone to find, after all!

"Where is it then?" she muttered, carefully lifting books and papers from Mia's desk, wondering if Mia might have hidden the phone underneath them. "Careful with that, Velvet!" she said, seeing the kitten batting playfully at a piece of paper.

But Velvet pushed the paper off the edge of the desk and Paige picked it up as it floated to the floor. She put it back on the table.

"I can't see my phone *anywhere*," Summer sighed, lifting up Mia's pillow to look underneath it. "She must have it with her."

Paige pulled open Mia's desk drawers and peered inside them. "Maybe you're right. I can't see it around here either," she murmured. "Oh, Velvet! Not again!"

The kitten had mischievously pushed the paper with her nose and sent it floating off the desk again. Paige picked it up and gave it a curious glance. "Velvet seems to be very taken with this paper," she commented, glancing at it. "It's a letter to Mia."

"What does it say?" Shannon asked, coming over to see.

Paige shook her head. "I'm not going to read Mia's private letters," she said, putting it back on the desk. But as she put the letter down, her eye was caught by a word on the sheet of paper: *Titania*. Paige paused, her hand still on the paper. "Wait a minute," she said slowly. "What's this?"

Despite a flash of guilt at reading Mia's letter, Paige couldn't help herself. She scanned it quickly, and gave a low whistle. "Listen to this," she said to the others. "It's from Mia's mum." She read aloud. "'Dear Mia, I can't tell you how proud I was when I read your letter, telling me that you've been picked to play Queen Titania . . .'"

Summer looked quizzical. "But she *wasn't* picked to—"

"Exactly!" Paige said. She read on. "'Did you know that Titania was the very role that first launched me as an actress?'"

Shannon nodded slowly. "It's all falling into place," she said thoughtfully. "Mia lied to her mum – presumably because she didn't want to disappoint her – and then . . ."

"And then, when she realized she wasn't going to be able to get away with her lie, she tried to get the play cancelled," Paige finished. She put the letter down on the desk, feeling stunned. "So Mia's been trying to sabotage the play, so that it wouldn't go ahead."

"And so that her mum wouldn't find out that she hadn't been picked as Titania!" Summer finished, open-mouthed. "Wow!"

"She must have felt such pressure to live up to her mum's success," Paige said, feeling a pang of sympathy.

"But it still seems pretty extreme – wrecking props, tearing up costumes . . ." Shannon said, shaking her head.

"She must have been desperate for her mum not to find out," Summer put in.

The girls stood in silence for a moment. Paige didn't agree with what Mia had done, but she was beginning to understand why the other girl had been so determined to stop the play from going ahead.

But at that moment, Velvet gave a loud *miaow* of warning, and darted under the nearest bed. Before the girls could react, though, the door opened and Abigail walked in.

"I can't believe I forgot my maths book!" she was muttering to herself – but then she jumped in surprise at the sight of Paige, Shannon and Summer.

"What . . . ?" she began bemusedly. Then she frowned. "What are you doing in here? You're not supposed to go into other people's dorms without permission," she reminded the girls angrily. "I'm going to tell Miss Linnet, right now!"

Chapter Eleven

Paige and her friends stared at each other in dismay and then chased after Abigail as she slammed out of the room. "Wait, Abigail!" Shannon shouted. "We had a good reason to be in there!"

But Abigail didn't break her stride as she ran downstairs. Her voice floated up to them, echoing in the stairwell. "Tell it to Miss Linnet!"

"Oh, no," Summer sighed. "Come back, Abigail. We can explain!"

"We'll just have to tell Miss Linnet the truth," Paige panted, as the three of them rushed after Abigail. "I'm sure she'll believe us." Paige was trying to sound reassuring and confident, but inside she wasn't so sure. Miss Linnet was very strict about her students respecting one another's privacy. She wasn't going to be at all pleased that Paige and her friends had been caught in someone else's dorm room.

By the time Paige, Summer and Shannon caught up with Abigail, she had already arrived at the head's office and the school secretary was in the process of ringing through to Miss Linnet. After a short conversation, she looked up at Abigail and nodded. "Miss Linnet will see you now," she said, opening the office door.

"We're coming too," Shannon said quickly, slipping in behind Abigail. Paige and Summer followed her.

Abigail shrugged. "I doubt it will make much difference," she said and strode confidently into the headteacher's office.

Miss Linnet was sitting at her desk. She looked surprised to see four, slightly out of breath, girls tumbling into her office. "Is everybody all right?" she asked. "Shouldn't you four be in a lesson?"

"Yes, we should," Abigail replied smartly.

"And that's where *I* was, until I realized I'd forgotten my maths book. So I went back to my room – only to find these three nosing around in there, without permission!"

"We weren't nosing around!" Shannon said hotly. "We were looking for—"

Miss Linnet held up a hand for silence. "Thank you for reporting this to me, Abigail. You may now return to your maths lesson."

"But—" Abigail protested. She obviously wanted to see Paige and her friends get told off, Paige thought in annoyance.

Miss Linnet raised an eyebrow and Abigail fell silent, blushing. "Is there anything else, Abigail?" Miss Linnet enquired.

Abigail shook her head. "No, miss," she said, and left the room.

Miss Linnet turned her gaze upon Paige, Shannon and Summer. "I am sure you are well aware that going into other girls' rooms without permission is strictly forbidden at Charm Hall," she said coolly. "Perhaps you could explain what you were doing in Abigail's room, when you should have been in your lesson."

Paige felt her cheeks grow hot at the stern note in the head's voice. She took a deep breath. "Miss Linnet, we *can* explain, I promise, but Mia should be here too," she said.

Miss Linnet looked a little surprised at Paige's words, but nodded. "Mia West? Very well," she said, and buzzed through to her secretary. "Could you have Mia West sent to my office, please?" she asked.

It seemed to take an age for Mia to arrive, and Paige began to feel sick with nerves as the minutes ticked by. This was horrible! She really hoped Mia would confess everything to Miss Linnet.

At last, there was a gentle knock at the door, and Mia came in, looking rather apprehensive.

"Ahh, Mia, good," Miss Linnet said briskly. "Now that you're here, perhaps somebody could tell me what's been going on."

There was an awkward silence. Mia fiddled nervously with her fingers, her cheeks pink, but she didn't say a word. Clearly, she wasn't planning on volunteering anything, Paige realized in dismay.

"We were looking for something," Shannon said after a few moments, with a fierce glance at Mia. "And Mia knows what."

Miss Linnet gave Shannon a long, appraising look. "Let me get this right. You three were looking for something in Abigail Carter's dorm—"

"It's Mia's dorm as well," Summer put in swiftly, and then looked down, blushing furiously.

Miss Linnet turned to Mia. "Well?" she asked, her voice getting steelier by the minute. "Mia, enlighten me. What might the girls have been doing in your room?"

Mia looked at the floor. "I . . . I don't know," she said nervously.

Miss Linnet sighed. "This is getting us nowhere," she said, fanning herself with a piece of paper. "Will somebody please tell me what's going on?"

Paige was feeling hot, too. This was not going at all well. It was clear that Miss Linnet's patience was fast running out.

The head stood up and went over to open a window. "Maybe some fresh air will clear your heads and loosen your tongues," she said, throwing the window open. "I certainly hope so, because if I don't get to the bottom of this soon I'm afraid I shall just have to put you all in detention!"

Just as she finished speaking, Velvet suddenly

jumped up on to the window sill.

"Oh!" Miss Linnet said in surprise. "It's that kitten again!"

Paige couldn't help smiling to herself as she remembered the chaos Velvet had caused hurtling around Miss Linnet's office. It had all ended happily though because, thanks to Velvet's antics, they had found an old legal document that had saved the entire school from closure. Still, Miss Linnet clearly wasn't ready to welcome Velvet back into her office just yet.

Miss Linnet turned back to face the girls, as Velvet sat down on the window sill and looked in at them all curiously.

"Now," said the head. "Where were we? Ah, yes. I was waiting for someone to tell me . . ."

Miss Linnet's voice faded away for Paige as she suddenly noticed a faint golden glimmer appear around Velvet's whiskers. As she watched, the kitten's whiskers started to vibrate and shimmer and the golden glow grew stronger. *What magic is Velvet about to do now?* Paige wondered excitedly.

Suddenly, the ringtone of a mobile phone filled the office, making everyone jump.

Paige recognized the familiar ringtone immediately and she grinned at Velvet. The clever kitten had somehow set Summer's phone ringing.

Mia clutched her blazer pocket, a surprised look on her face. Everyone watched as Mia took the phone out of her pocket. "Sorry," she mumbled. "I thought I'd switched it off."

"I'll have that, please," Miss Linnet said, sounding annoyed. "You know very well that you should not be carrying a phone around with you during lesson time."

Mia handed over Summer's phone, and Velvet promptly jumped down from the window sill and disappeared into the garden. The phone stopped ringing at once.

"Kittens, phones, whatever next?" Miss Linnet sighed. "Come on, girls, I don't have all day. What were you three doing in Mia's room? Just tell me."

Paige and her friends exchanged a look. Miss Linnet was actually holding the proof that showed exactly what Mia had done. Paige knew that they could just tell the head the whole story, but she couldn't help thinking it would be much better if

Mia confessed. She wanted Mia to have one last chance. But Mia was silent.

At last, Shannon spoke. "We were looking for a book that Mia had asked us to fetch," Shannon said smoothly. Paige spotted her crossing her fingers behind her back. "Weren't we, Mia?" Shannon added, turning to Mia with a meaningful look.

Mia turned scarlet. She looked very surprised – and grateful – that they hadn't mentioned the phone or the photo on it, Paige thought. She nodded firmly. "It's true, Miss Linnet," Mia said clearly. "I asked them to get my maths textbook for me."

Miss Linnet didn't seem entirely satisfied with this explanation. "Hmm," she mused. "I get the feeling that there's something you're not telling me, girls, but if you're all sticking to this story, then so be it. Mia, you can come back for this phone at the end of the day. And don't let me catch you with it during school hours again!"

"No, Miss Linnet, you won't," Mia said, looking down at the floor.

"Now, I want all of you to get back to class straight away," Miss Linnet instructed. "Tell Mrs

Stark that you've been with me."

The four girls nodded and trooped out of the office.

"I'm sorry I took your phone," Mia muttered to Summer. "And thanks for not telling Miss Linnet that I did."

Paige decided to get straight to the point. "Mia, when we were searching for Summer's phone, I saw a letter from your mum in your room," she said awkwardly. "And . . . and we read it."

Mia shuffled her feet, looking very unhappy. "So you know what I told my mum, then," she said in a low voice. "That I lied and said that I had been picked to play Titania."

"Yes," Paige said gently. "We know."

There was a moment of silence, and then Mia sniffed. "Nobody understands how hard it is, trying to follow in her footsteps," she confessed. "Everyone expects so much of me – Diana West's daughter!" She sighed. "I just couldn't tell her that I hadn't been given the part, that I wasn't good enough. That's why I lied."

"And I guess that's why you were sabotaging the play. You wanted it to be cancelled," Shannon said.

Mia nodded. "Yes," she agreed in a hoarse voice, looking away.

"Oh, Mia, what a mess," Summer said kindly, putting a hand on Mia's arm.

"I know," Mia agreed. She scrubbed at her eyes with her fists. "But I didn't know what else to do. I panicked."

"Well, you'll have to tell Miss Collins that," Shannon said. "If you tell her what you've told us, she'll understand. But you have to own up to what you did."

Mia nodded miserably. "I know," she said. "And I need to tell my mum, too. I'll go and do it after maths."

Paige smiled at her encouragingly. She felt glad that the mystery had been unravelled, but sad for Mia that she'd got into such a panic over the play.

"Come on," Shannon said with a wry smile. "Let's get back to maths before we get into any more trouble today."

That evening at dinner, Miss Collins stood up at the front of the dining hall. "I have a brief announcement to make," she said. "And it's good news. Someone has owned up to damaging the play's costumes. They have explained to me why they did such a thing. I'm quite convinced now that they won't be causing any further problems. So I'm pleased to say that the play is back on!"

There was a loud cheer at the news. Everybody looked delighted.

"And Mia has very kindly agreed to work around the clock to make a new dress for Queen Titania," Miss Collins added. Paige noticed Miss Collins and Mia share a look of understanding.

"Hurrah!" cheered Paige along with everyone else. "The show *will* go on!"

Chapter Twelve

"Good luck," Paige said to Summer, hugging her carefully so as not to crush her wings.

"You'll be great," Shannon added, coming to hug Summer too. "Break a leg – but not literally, all right?"

Summer laughed and began warming up her muscles by stretching her arms and legs. Tonight was the first performance of the play, and there were just ten minutes to go before the curtain went up.

The last few weeks had passed by in a blur of rehearsals, costume-fittings and finishing touches to the scenery and props. It was hard work, but a lot of fun. Paige could hardly believe that they had finished everything in time. Now, the assembly hall was full to the rafters with parents and girls, all waiting for the show to begin.

In the dressing room, there was a nervous buzz as the actors had their hair and make-up done, and their costumes checked for any last-minute alterations. Priya was muttering Titania's lines into the mirror, with a fierce look of concentration on her face. Kelly, who was playing King Oberon, was fiddling anxiously with her crown and pacing up and down. And Ellie, who was playing Lysander, was worrying that her moustache would fall off on stage and kept asking Miss Henry, who was doing everybody's make-up, to put on some extra glue!

Miss Collins bustled up, looking a little nervous, her cheeks flushed. "I just want to say you've been a wonderful team," she told the girls. "I'm sure it's going to be a fantastic night, and that you're all going to turn in great performances!" She smiled. "Just five minutes now until the show starts, so break a leg, everyone!"

Time seemed to speed up after that. All the girls

who'd been working behind the scenes went into the assembly hall to take their seats. And then the play began!

Paige felt nervous and proud all at once when the curtains opened and she saw the actors in front of the scenery she herself had helped to paint. A hushed silence fell as the first characters, Theseus and Hippolyta, began speaking in clear voices. Although she knew the play really well by now, it wasn't long before Paige herself was lost in the story, laughing at naughty Puck and clapping at Summer's gymnastics, just like everyone else.

When the curtain finally fell, everyone got to their feet and the hall rang with the sound of their applause. Paige and Shannon clapped happily along with everyone else, delighted that the audience had enjoyed the show as much as they had.

The applause died down after a few minutes, as Miss Linnet came on stage, smiling broadly.

"I'm sure you'll all agree with me when I say what a wonderful performance that was!" she said. "You've seen for yourselves what talented actors we have at Charm Hall, but we also need to applaud all those hard-working girls who helped out behind the scenes. There are too many people for me to mention them all individually, but perhaps I could say a few special thank-yous. First of all, to our stage manager, Abigail Carter, and our assistant director, Shannon Carroll. Come on stage, girls!"

There was another huge round of applause as Abigail and Shannon hurried up and on to the stage next to Miss Linnet, flushed and smiling.

Miss Linnet went on to mention several of the prop makers, the sound and lighting girls, and then thanked Paige, Alice and Louisa too, for all their work on the scenery. Paige felt herself blushing furiously as she walked up the aisle towards the stage, especially when she saw her parents turning around in their seats to see her, clapping and smiling.

Paige joined the others on stage to take her applause. Then, as they all filed off again, she was sure she saw a pair of wide amber eyes watching her from the shadows of the wings. It was Velvet, she was certain. In fact, Paige had a feeling that the little kitten had seen the entire play.

"Finally, a big thank you to Mia West and her team for designing and making all the fabulous costumes," Miss Linnet went on. "I'm sure you'll all agree that Mia has a real gift for design." Her eyes twinkled as she sought out Mia in the audience and gestured for her to come up on stage. "Maybe we have the next Stella McCartney with us right here at Charm Hall!"

A very pleased-looking Mia came on stage, and Paige spotted Mia's mum clapping enthusiastically

in the audience. Diana West couldn't have looked any prouder if she'd tried!

After the play, there was a party for the Year Five pupils and their families and friends who had come to watch the play. Paige bounded up to her parents and threw her arms around them. "Mum! Dad!" she cried happily. "It's *so* nice to see you again!"

Her parents hugged her tightly.

"I loved the play," Paige's mum said, kissing the top of her head.

"Your backdrops were brilliant," her dad added affectionately. "I had no idea you were so talented." He grinned. "When we move back to England again, you can help with the decorating."

Paige laughed. "Come and meet Summer and Shannon," she urged. "They're my best friends, and they're just over here."

"The famous Summer and Shannon," Mrs Hart said with a smile as Paige introduced her mum to her friends. "Hello, girls. I've heard a lot about you two from Paige."

"All good, I hope," Shannon said, grinning at Paige's parents.

Paige introduced her parents to some of her teachers. Then, while Mr and Mrs Hart were chatting to some of the other parents, Paige went back to find her friends.

As the girls queued for lemonade, they saw Mia with her mum. "Titania's dress' was wonderful," Diana West was saying proudly. "Much nicer than the one I had to wear when I played the part!" She hugged Mia. "I can't believe you made such a beautiful thing, Mia. You *are* clever, sweetheart!"

Mia beamed with pride, and Paige felt pleased for her. After all Mia's worries, it looked as if her mum didn't mind at all that she hadn't been picked to play Titania.

Later on, when the party had ended and Paige had said goodbye to her parents, she went up to her dorm, with Shannon and Summer, to get ready for bed.

"What a wonderful day!" Paige sighed, sitting down on her bed.

There was a little *miaow* from under Shannon's desk, and Velvet suddenly appeared. She jumped up on to Paige's bed, purring happily.

"Oh, Velvet, did you enjoy the play too?" Paige asked, stroking the kitten. "I'm glad you came to watch."

Shannon and Summer came over to stroke Velvet as well.

"Today's been even better than wonderful," Shannon said, thoughtfully. "It's been *magical!*"

Paige grinned at her friends. "And it's all down to Velvet the witch cat!" she said.

Shannon nodded and Summer kissed Velvet on the top of her furry head.

"Hurrah for Velvet!" laughed Summer.

"Yes, hurrah for Velvet!" cheered Paige and Shannon together.

If you want to read more
about the **magic** at
Charm Hall, then
turn over for the start of
the next adventure ...

Chapter One

"Hello, everyone! I'm back!"

Paige Hart burst into her dorm room at Charm Hall Boarding School, her auburn hair flying, and a huge grin on her face. She'd been looking forward to this moment ever since she'd said goodbye to her mum and dad at the airport in Dubai.

Shannon Carroll and Summer Kirby, Paige's best friends, were standing by their beds unpacking their suitcases. But when they saw Paige, they both dropped the piles of clothes they were holding and dashed across the room, yelling out a greeting.

"Oh, Paige, it's great to see you!" Shannon

declared, grabbing her friend in a bearhug. "Did you have a good time in Dubai?"

"Ooh, you're so brown, Paige!" Summer laughed. "I'm *really* jealous."

Paige grinned. "Dubai was great, but it's brilliant to be back!" she exclaimed.

It was hard for Paige to believe that, last term, when her dad had suddenly been sent to Dubai for his work, she hadn't wanted to come to Charm Hall. Today, when Paige had arrived back at the beautiful old manor house again, it had felt just like coming home. "Where's Velvet?" she asked eagerly.

As she spoke, Paige felt something furry brush against her legs, and she looked down to see the small jet-black kitten at her feet. Velvet was purring loudly and staring up at Paige with her warm golden eyes.

"Hello, Velvet!" Paige said, sweeping the kitten up into her arms. "I've missed you!"

Velvet purred even louder, and pushed her nose against Paige's cheek.

"I know you liked Dubai, but I bet you didn't meet any magical kittens, like Velvet, out there!" Shannon teased.

Paige laughed. The three girls had found out about Velvet's magical powers during the previous term. The kitten had arrived in their dorm room one stormy afternoon, and Paige, Summer and Shannon had soon realized that Velvet was no ordinary cat.

"I'd better start unpacking," Paige said, putting Velvet gently down on the floor. Her suitcase had been sent on ahead and was already lying on her bed. "I've got presents for you all from Dubai!"

"Ooh, I love presents!" gasped Shannon.

Velvet leaped up on to Paige's bed and sniffed curiously at the suitcase as Paige threw back the lid.

"These are for you!" Paige told her friends, holding out two giftbags.

Shannon and Summer took the bags and peered inside. They both grinned at Paige when they saw the silver bangles she'd brought them.

"Thanks, Paige!" they said together.

"I got some sweets for Joan as well," Paige added. "To thank her for feeding Velvet while we were away.' Joan was one of the school dinner ladies. She had seen Velvet around the school grounds and assumed that the kitten was from a nearby farm.

She knew the girls fed Velvet and so she had offered to carry on doing so while the girls were away over the summer. Joan didn't know Velvet lived in the girls' dorm though. That was a big secret, because pets weren't allowed at Charm Hall.

Meanwhile, Velvet had jumped into Paige's suitcase and was padding around on top of the clothes, sniffing curiously.

"Yes, I've got something for you, too, Velvet!" Paige laughed. She rooted around in the case and held up a pink mouse attached to a long golden string. Velvet fixed the mouse with an intent gaze, and then leaped at it as Paige swung it above her head.

"Velvet's getting a bit spoiled!" Shannon remarked, shaking her head as Velvet continued to bat the mouse to and fro. "She's got so many toys! Summer's brought her a little ball with a bell inside."

"And what about *you*?" Summer demanded, laughing. "*You* bought her a box of treats!"

Shannon grinned and glanced at Velvet, who, having just knocked her mouse to the floor, was getting ready to pounce. "Well, the supermarket at home had a much bigger selection than the shop at the end of the school drive," she said. "And Velvet's mad about her treats!"

Paige began unpacking, and Summer and Shannon went back to their own suitcases.

"Oh, I've brought this too.' Shannon held up a silver torch and waved it in the air. "Now we'll be able to see what we're eating when we have our midnight feasts!"

"Great idea, Shannon," agreed Summer. "My phone torch didn't give us enough light. Do you remember when I dropped that big bag of crisps and they went all over the floor? We were crawling around for ages, trying to see to pick them all up!"

Paige and Shannon laughed.

"Well, we'll have a *fantastic* midnight feast tonight," said Shannon, waving some chocolate bars.

Paige heaved a happy sigh. A new term at Charm Hall was starting and she had a feeling it was going to be just as much fun as the last.

"You know what you were saying yesterday, about how great it is to be back at Charm Hall?" Shannon whispered to Paige the next morning after breakfast. The girls were on their way to a special assembly to welcome everyone back to school.

Paige nodded, looking puzzled.

"Well," Shannon went on in a low voice, "not even Charm Hall's perfect!" And she nodded at the group of girls in front of them.

"Oh, I'm *so* glad we didn't go to boring old Spain!" Abigail Carter was saying to her dorm-mates, Mia and Chloe. "My parents took me to Florida for two weeks, and we stayed in a *really* posh hotel."

Paige pulled a face at Shannon and Summer. Abigail Carter was in their form, and she was a *major* pain.

"I'd forgotten all about Abigail," Paige said with a grin.

"Lucky you!" Summer winked at her.

The girls entered the hall and Paige looked round at the high, arched windows and the wood-panelled walls.

Then Shannon nudged her. "Check out the newbie teacher," she whispered to Paige and Summer. "Just behind Miss Collins."

Paige tried to glance over her shoulder without being too obvious. There was a woman she'd never seen before sitting just behind their English teacher. She had black hair drawn back off her face, and green eyes.

"Maybe she's our new history teacher," Summer suggested. "Miss Gordon left at the end of last term "

But the girls didn't have time to speculate any more as Miss Linnet, the headmistress, swept into the hall at that very moment. Silence fell as she mounted the stage.

"Welcome back, girls!" Miss Linnet began with a smile. "I can't tell you how pleased I am to see you all here for the new term at Charm Hall. I am *especially* pleased after the events of last term!"

Paige glanced at Summer and Shannon. The school had been on the verge of closing, due to part of Lavinia Charm's will being lost. The vital piece of paper which meant that the school could stay open had finally been found because of Velvet.

"Before we begin, I would like to welcome two new members of staff," Miss Linnet went on. "We have a new caretaker, Sam Morris, whom I'm sure you will see around the grounds."

Everyone, including Paige, Summer and

Shannon, looked round to see a middle-aged man with grey-streaked dark hair and steady brown eyes sitting at the back of the hall.

"We also have a new history teacher," Miss Linnet continued. "Mrs Stockbridge." The head smiled at the woman the three friends had been looking at. "I know you'll both enjoy your time here."

"I wonder what Mrs Stockbridge is like," Shannon whispered to Paige.

Paige was about to reply when she saw Miss Collins staring crossly at them, so she kept quiet.

"A new school year is always a wonderful time," Miss Linnet said. "It's the beginning of new adventures and new challenges. And this year, I would like to start things off with a bang!" She paused and looked around the hall. Everyone was hanging on the head's every word.

"And so," Miss Linnet continued, "I'm very pleased to tell you that we are going to have a big Hallowe'en party at the end of October!"

**With magic in the air at Charm Hall,
this is one boarding school where
anything can happen!**

It's Christmas time and the choir enter a carol
competition. But then they find out another
school is singing the same carols!

Velvet takes Paige, Summer and Shannon
back in time to solve the mystery of why
the famous Mona Lisa is smiling and
they find a way to save the choir, too.

*Hodder
Children's
Books*

A division of Hachette Children's Books

With magic in the air at Charm Hall, this is one boarding school where anything can happen !

Paige can't believe she didn't want to come to Charm Hall now that she's met Summer and Shannon, her new best friends.

Then a black kitten mysteriously appears. She's so cute they don't have the heart to get rid of her, especially when she turns out to be more than just an average kitten!

Hodder
Children's
Books

A division of Hachette Children's Books

Charm Hall

Toil and Trouble

With magic in the air at Charm Hall, this is one boarding school where anything can happen!

A mysterious diary reveals to Paige, Summer and Shannon that a precious sapphire is hidden in the school grounds.

Then they discover someone is trying to steal the jewel! Can the girls – with Velvet's help - stop them in time

Hodder Children's Books

A division of Hachette Children's Books